A Cemetery for Bees

A Cemetery for Bees

a novel

ALINA DUMITRESCU

Translated by KATIA GRUBISIC

First published as *Le cimetière des abeilles* in 2016 by Éditions Triptyque, a division of Groupe Nota bene, Montreal.

Copyediting: Jennifer McMorran
Author photo: Louis Desjardins
Cover design: Debbie Geltner
Illustrations: Edwin Stanculescu
Cover image: Shutterstock
Book design: Tika eBooks

Library and Archives Canada Cataloguing in Publication

Title: A cemetery for bees : a novel / Alina Dumitrescu ; translated by Katia Grubisic.

Other titles: Cimetière des abeilles. English

Names: Dumitrescu, Alina, author. | Grubisic, Katia, translator.

Description: Translation of: Le cimetière des abeilles.

Identifiers: Canadiana (print) 20200337637 | Canadiana (ebook) 20200337734 | ISBN 9781773900834 (softcover) | ISBN 9781773900841 (EPUB) | ISBN 9781773900858 (Kindle) | ISBN 9781773900865 (PDF)

Classification: LCC PS8607.U4444 C5613 2021 | DDC C843/.6—dc23

Printed and bound in Canada.

The publisher gratefully acknowledges the support of the Government of Canada through the Canada Council for the Arts, the Canada Book Fund, and of the Government of Quebec through the Société de développement des entreprises culturelles (SODEC).

We acknowledge the financial support of the Government of Canada through the National Translation Program for Book Publishing, an initiative of the Action Plan for Official Languages - 2018-2023: Investing in Our Future, for our translation activities.

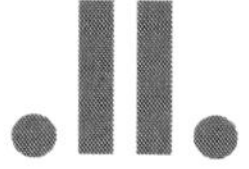

Linda Leith Publishing
Montreal
www.lindaleith.com

We think that when one thing ends
another begins right away.
No: between the two, it's chaos.

—Marguerite Duras

To the language genie.

For Andy.

For the big brothers; they know who they are.

On Meeting Monsieur de La Fontaine

Go to Paris, unmake the original mistake.

When it tried to drop me off at my parents' place in Romania, the stork was probably turned away, recipient unknown.

It could have taken me back, or made a detour. But the stork had no imagination, or it didn't speak the language, and was exhausted to boot.

Beckon other fairies to the cradle. Choose another language to cast the spell, not your childhood language.

There were years of dreaming and reading, about Paris, a bit about France, war films, or rather, romanticized films about war. Jacquard, the Lumière brothers, Bernard Palissy, Marie Curie, Blériot, Pasteur. For centuries, the French were the people who knew things—about God and cathedrals, about fabric, about marrying up (and down), about ships, laws, about art, about memory. And they've got that striking idiomatic flair.

Behind closed, impenetrable borders, I put on a show of my own.

The only time I was able to get out of the country was when I was nineteen, on the Romanian–Soviet Friendship Train. I told myself it was to prepare to leave for the West one day.

When I got off the train at the station in Moscow, my yearning for all things foreign was dealt a harsh blow: we were greeted with flags, a red carpet, and a brass band playing the *Internationale*.

Now, years later, I'm in France at last, the Parisian sky etched by the plane trees. As I turn onto a street toward the museum, another miracle; standing before me is none other than Jean de La Fontaine.

I curtsy low before him but he stays cold as stone, or bronze, actually, him and his fox, a book tucked under his arm, and the crow with the cheese. This is in the square du Ranelagh, in the 16e arrondissement.

I glance at the Sorbonne, where I'll never study. The facade is being renovated. Students in the street speak freely, in Romanian, even. This is the age of Erasmus.

I've arrived too late.

In a small local bookstore, I buy some ink and a notebook. Next door there's another bookstore, solely philosophical, lost in thought.

In the evening, we sip a Beaujolais nouveau on a terrasse, with *braseros* warming our calves. Very chic, very much of the West.

Perhaps I'm not too late after all. After all, there is a *nouveau* vintage every year.

The blood of France sings in my veins.

By the Eiffel Tower, Roma hawkers want to sell me knick-knacks. Their baubles of the tower cost three euros more than the same souvenirs in the official gift shop. We are far past autofiction. Even the Romani got here before me.

At the top of the tower, a glass of champagne. Love. It's such a cliché, as long as you don't take into account the actual lovers. Snapshot: a moment of eternity.

In the Eiffel Tower bathrooms there's a *dame pipi*, a toilet attendant like in old black and white films. She's knitting. I'm obviously not as late as I thought.

The rooftops are crowded with a terracotta army of Parisian chimneys.

I walk around aimlessly. I'm in Paris! The sidewalks are Parisian sidewalks. The fragrant October air takes me in its arms.

There are no book stalls along the banks of the Seine. *The Seine is lucky, she has no worries*. Prévert, old man, you're old news.

I'm in Paris and I'm breathing in *l'air du temps*. I am here now and my heart is overwhelmed, my heart is a wrought-iron balcony.

At the Ambassade d'Auvergne, we splurge on foie gras and aligot, quince brandy. I'm catching up.

I am thinking of the bronze gentleman and his fables; there's nothing to be gained by running if you don't start at the right time.

Coming out of the Odéon metro station, my gaze lands directly on Danton's genteel, expressive anatomy. The words on the statue's pedestal will resound forever: *After bread, education is the first need of the people*.

And so I leave behind the splendour of France as my journey, too short, ends.

On the plane, as I return to my slice of France in America, I promise myself that I will come back soon, for the plane trees, for the terracotta chimneys. The Paris sky.

Betwixt

This morning, when I wake up, my world is spinning on its axis just as it should, humming along as usual.

Those who know have spent the night sliding the right keys in the right locks, redrawing the borders, and reining in the hurricanes.

Before seven o'clock this morning, my world was still standing, all logic and harmony on rue Bayne in Montreal, Quebec.

In the tiny apartment, on weekdays, dictionaries line up by the cockroaches. To everything there is a season: the day is for dictionaries, the night for cockroaches. Weekends are less orderly, roaches and dictionaries frolicking in orgiastic chaos. Their spawn are words with three heads, spontaneous abortions, and, oh, the mess on Monday mornings.

During the day, orders are given in French, and at night, cockroaches meander around on their umpteen legs. Weekends are like dreams, filled with snippets of mixed languages and smells.

I fall asleep at home and wake up in the West—and in French, besides! French, the language of culture, the great one. French speaks of history, of humanity, of transcendence. For the more modest words of everyday life, I don't dare use French, that grande dame.

I am reduced to silence. Some mornings I wake up on the Romanian side and other days on the French side of the bed. Most often, my eyes half open, I wait under the blankets for a long time, in the middle of the jumble. Neither fish nor fowl, half French, half Romanian, my brain is bewildered by the effort of just getting to the words.

Do my dreams affect the language I wake up in?

Or maybe it's about what side of the bed I get up on? Left for French, the language of the left hand, the Left Bank, a bed left behind. Romanian is on the right side, where the rug at my feet makes getting up easier.

Linguistic quickening is a temporary state, a state of doubt, self-censorship.

Is it *puisque* or *parce que*, is it *bientôt* or *tantôt*—

since or because, soon or later?

Nostalgic echoes of a time when access to words was direct, instantaneous, luminous. Words used to be well behaved, waiting patiently for someone to lure them out. They recognized each other, called each other by name. Words knew their place, they waited their turn. When I was a child, sometimes they would even take the first step.

We spoke naturally, without any existential drama, we said *mom*, *dog*, *dad*, *gone*, and *give*. We were told *thank you* and *well done*.

Speaking was like breathing, like seeing or eating. It just was, there was no ulterior motive.

Yet all it took was a foreign visitor or a subtitled film, a language class, the slightest trace of migration. Confusion, revelation! All at once you were no longer merely speaking, you were speaking a particular language.

During holidays on the Black Sea, the beach was full of Germans, Italians, and Scandinavians. They were beautiful, sculpted by the light glinting off their perfumed tanning oil. I watched, alert, taking in the foreign smells, none of which my nostrils had ever sampled before. I craved the exotic.

The tourists from away wore colourful bathing suits and stylish sunglasses. Even their wrinkles were different from our parents' wrinkles. They must have had other worries, which traced other lines on their faces.

We spoke with them in a kind of foreignese. Most of the time, a little French was enough.

The foreigners on the beach were as worthy of admiration as the Black Sea itself. Plus they had chocolate.

Guerlain in America

My brother is one of those who know. Like other worldly types, he understands the mechanics, how to work the system, the keys and the locks, how to set the earth in motion for another day.

From time to time, the cogs get dirty—deep in the heart of the earth, where some people think hell is, because of volcanoes.

While I sleep, those who know how to keep the earth turning do what they have to do.

When I wake, everything is already buzzing. The sun is in its place, planes slip by high in the sky. The dying are dying, babies are being born, the milk has been delivered.

I live on the inflation of words. The vocabulary of abundance. The lexicon of happiness. These are the trademarks of the West. Guerlain perfume, Guerlain in America.

America is a swindle. Europeans only changed their names a little; Jews too.

My house in exile overlooks the highway. There are no hives, no lilacs, no bees. There's one bee, actually, the stylized bee embossed on the perfume bottle: Aqua Allegoria *mandarine basilic*, Guerlain, Paris. In the morning, at seven o'clock, the fullness and the void must be carefully maintained. This is my world, a honeycomb, full of passageways to the other side of the earth. Canals, remembrances.

How often the details disappear, tiny holes swallowed within the larger gears. Those who know, the chosen among the chosen, are out at dawn with their spanners, their wrenches, their streetlight snuffers.

As day breaks, there is a moment of disarray, objects take on a blurry, milky outline.

Every morning of my new life, I drink my coffee with two slices of maple-flavoured autofiction, which make my life bearable.

Life is sprinkled with words that point to realities that are unlived, untouchable, words about desire, about material possession.

Guerlain parfumeur. I live in the opulence of words. *Évanescence. Entre la poire et le fromage. Apéritif, incongru*. Between the pears and the cheese, one thing and another.

The word as perfect epitaph. Finally, something conclusive from the afterlife—words consigned to eternity.

The wizards—those who know—make the words throb with other words, and silences with silence.

Without too much hassle, in the powerful gears of modernity, they manage to make the emptiness line up with the emptiness and the fullness with the fullness.

The highway is always there, rushing through the hours, the highway of rat-racers in their cars and in trucks, *ad perpetuam*, beyond the triple-pane windows.

My bee is alone, frozen on the perfume bottle. Guerlain, Paris. Shoved into its white honeycombed box, the bottle's only function is to pour a little perfume, a little hope and luxury, into my daily grind.

I'm cut off from my native language upstream and down. My mother tongue shrinks until it becomes just my mother's tongue.

My mother, who cannot pronounce the letters *u*, *n*, or *e* in French. As a child, I withdrew into my head to escape her. Now I take refuge in French. I turn away, I turn a deaf ear by writing in a language she can't read or understand. Linguistic revenge.

And—a second, involuntary revenge—my children can't read Romanian, they understand only a few words. Romanian is their mother's tongue. I'm the only person who speaks Romanian to them, and most of the time we talk to each other in French. My sons speak French to each other, and also the language of movies, computers, secrets. So many languages that are inaccessible to me.

Between my mother and my children, I am lost, in one direction a linguistic orphan, and in the other, bereaved.

It's an impossible situation, but language dries up when it's not used, just like memories dry up when they're not remembered, revisited.

The mother tongue, which becomes the mother's tongue, which becomes a dead language, dead to us. This is the primal shock of immigration.

My sons can't taste the subtleties of the language that cradled me, and through which I came to French. My sons are strangers to me, sacrificed for a better life, a radiant future. I have stepped out of the ranks, out of my lineage, my continent too. As the old defection joke goes, you search elsewhere to see if you're there.

Most of the time I'm not. Travelling back to the old country, I find that I am missing. My lilac bush has withered and grown sparse, it no longer knows me. And I can't quite find myself in my adopted country either. It's a double absence. My roots are ambivalent, growing in the shape of a crown, upside down. Aerial roots.

A few childhood songs, stories, cadences, and nursery rhymes, flimsy barricades against oblivion. My mother's book of recipes is a light in the darkness; that, and an alphabet book.

On my list, for my ark, I ask, who will be saved? Which word, which story? They let me leave with only two suitcases. Two suitcases and the child. The furniture was sold, the jewellery sold or given away, the carpets abandoned to the moths, to mothopoesis.

The perpetual saint

KEEPSAKES

Panopticon

I used to take the shortest path to words; all you had to do was reach out and grab what you wanted. At the very top of the tower, the restless, all-seeing eye. On the altar, fruit, wheat, and wood.

Already my children have lost the language, or at least they speak very little. Only prayers and hymns, and the language of anger. What are their dreams made of? What word means nostalgia to them? What colour is the colour of fear, a cry, the smell of wood? Before the memories dry up I should dip a quill in my blood. My anagrammatic childhood, my aerial roots. My life elsewhere is like a tree's sap diverted, a destiny unfulfilled. My life elsewhere, so poor, below the threshold of what is translatable.

I used to know the shortest path to words; all I

had to do was reach out and there they were, like pieces of bread. All I had to do was dip my head to quench my thirst.

At the top of the tower, the eye. On the altar, the dictionary. Auto-da-fé.

The memory smells scorched. My village had everything: mountains and children, bread and stories. We had Greeks, Macedonians, Roma, the hospital, the school, the bread factory. At seven o'clock, the factory's siren would sound, reminding us that school was about to start.

The old Jew would give my brother and me a coin, one leu. He was the watchmaker. He wore checkered trousers. On the Sabbath, he took his pocket watch out for a walk along the main street, the chain dangling. It doesn't matter that we were Protestant; like him, we kept the Sabbath. Instead of Sunday like everyone else, we went to church on Saturdays, washed and starched and told to behave. The watchmaker went to synagogue.

At the top of the tower the eye never closes, evil eye.

Our village had a hermaphrodite, about whom unbelievable stories were whispered in the schoolyard and the washroom.

We had a madwoman, fat, with a flowery dress and pearl necklace, white face, black hair, a red mouth like a wound, Pakitzanka.

We had a one-legged man, our obligatory war hero begging in the street, his voice nasal, his hat made of holes and medals. We egged each other on; who among us children would dare give him something to eat? I gave him black bread, or an onion, sometimes a little money.

The farmer and his donkey, selling us potatoes at the market. We would sneak up to his cart and hang off the back, giggling nervously as we waited to be found out and given a whipping.

We had our market, in the middle of the town, a market like any other. Concrete counters with fish, fruit, vegetables, herbs, cheeses wrapped in vine leaves, woven baskets. They looked like mortuary tables—especially for the fish, dissected under running water.

The fruits of the earth: *welcome everything that comes to you*!

We had a matching widow and orphan, a pederast, a pious woman, a deaf and mute painter and, yes, in the middle of the park, our Monument to the Unknown Soldier.

I used to take a secret passage to get to the sounds; all I had to do was reach out my hand to get my bread. From the top of the tower, the restless eye. On the altar, the ear. Auto-da-fé.

★

I used to know the path to get to the words; all I had to do was reach out my hand to get my bread. I used to understand the language of the chamomile bees. The unclosing eye at the top of the hill.

My village had everything: an Orthodox church, a Catholic church, a Protestant church, a synagogue. The burial grounds were a bit more complicated. The Jewish cemetery, fine. The Orthodox and Catholic cemeteries, yes. But where did Protestants bury their dead? We weren't allowed to have a cemetery, so we died as little as possible, we didn't want to bother anyone. When you couldn't stand it anymore, you died anyway, just a little.

And then they would bury us on the edge of the cemetery, with the unbaptized children, the Roma, and the suicides.

At each funeral we attended, we would go visit the children's graves, the surprising dead, their two-day lives, two weeks. Wooden crosses, whitewashed. The wind and rain faded the names so quickly, in two days, two weeks.

At the top of the tower, the restless eye. On the altar, memory. Auto-da-fé.

★

My village had everything: oil, salt, a stateless man, the museum, mineral springs, a railway station. *Gară*, the sign read, *terminus*.

With my little blue faded suitcase, I mingled with the travellers who were arriving, hoping for some travel to rub off on me. I watched them, their clothes, their luggage, their attitude, their cameras. I tried to look nonchalant and slightly disillusioned, as if I were travelling too. And then I hurried back before my parents got home.

My older brother went off to the army. Papa made him a suitcase of brown lacquered wood, which smelled like fresh burial paint. One last family photo before he had to shave his head. Childhood, *terminus*.

I used to know the path to words so easily. There was nothing in the way, all I had to do was reach out my hand to get my bread and bend to drink from the spring.

The Roma buried their dead on Thursdays, their brass bands blasting happy tunes through the air. I've always felt that Thursday burials don't count.

The Roma got married on Thursdays too. The same brass band kept the whole village awake until dawn. I don't think Thursday weddings count either.

★

My village has everything, a pharmacy, a stadium, a movie theatre, a newsstand. The armless woman at the newsstand knits with her feet, combs her hair with her feet. Poised and polished, she gives us our change.

A visitor comes. He stays with the neighbours. He is Black. He has chewing gum, chocolate, a foreign passport, and he speaks a foreign language. I show him my treasures, my Pioneer tie and my pins, hoping to exchange them for a bit of gum. But he doesn't get it.

In my grade-two class, the children are blond with blue eyes. They've never seen a passport or chewing gum, and they've certainly never seen any Black people. I explain to the visitor, with elaborate gestures and the few French words I know, that I would like to take him to school. This time he understands. I take him by the hand and bring him to school. There's a commotion, whispers. *He's black, he's all black!* The teachers turn red. I didn't ask permission before bringing a visitor to school. I don't get detention, this time.

My teacher carefully averts a diplomatic incident.

And for months and months after, the kids talk about him, saying that the visitor's skin was white under his shirt, that his blackness ends at his shirt collar and cuffs, like a 1930s jazzman inside out.

★

My village had everything. The only things that were imported were Russian watches, the Protestant faith, olives, the magnolia trees in front of the hospital, Chinese fountain pens, German cameras, the Blue Rose of Russia, oranges and lemons, communism.

Everything else we had: grandmothers, coffee mills, bread, local patriotism, a piano, a loom, teachers, a doctor, a hill, a seamstress, the paint seller (with a white beard and rainbow hair), fir trees, legends, a fortune teller, a madman, a soup kitchen, a shoemaker.

Everything, bees and honey, a flag, illusions, mineral water, the painter.

Of what we imported, I liked the oranges and lemons. They were packed in tissue paper and kept their smell for a long time. *Jaffa*, the paper read.

I remember I used to live all year round in the

secret passage that leads straight to the words, a rose is a rose is a rose is a rose. All I had to do was reach out my hand to touch the bread, lift my foot to dance, tilt my head slightly to shatter the surface of the water. Sweet apple juice, warm and sour at the back of the throat, flowed plain and clear. An apple is an apple is an apple is an apple.

At the top of the tower is Gertrude Stein's eye. On the altar, some wheat, Tristan Tzara's bowtie, a handful of ashes.

Once a year, in the fall, the circus came to town.

At War With the Turks

This afternoon, my big brother is going to war against the Turks, over there, behind the hill. The battlefield is no place for little girls, everyone knows that. Eleven-year-old boys are a different story.

All afternoon, I play both widow and orphan, my sticky hands clasped together, praying for my brother to come back victorious from his war with the Turks. Victorious, and especially alive.

I'm starting to get hungry. Where are the parents when it really matters?

I press my hands against the front of my overalls, on my olive-green-velvet–striped belly. I'm hungry, but I must to keep watch. My life depends on it. Words lose their meaning. I'm filled with panicky foreboding: meaning, quickly, I must have meaning. I ask the Almighty, the Most

High, please, my brother, the Turks, keep him alive. I'm hungry, my brother, the sun, the hill, the Almighty, who lives—no, who art in heaven, I'm hungry. May he be alive, forever, don't leave me alone with our parents.

There's nothing, no one else between me and my parents. What if they suddenly realize that? Our Father who art in heaven, I won't steal any more cherries from the neighbours, keep him alive... My belly striped in olive velvet... I'm hungry!

★

Our parents call us to dinner. I could kiss him, but I don't have time. *Your hands are dirty*. We have to wash our hands before we eat. *Take your elbows off the table! Who's saying grace?* Not me! My brother has nary a scratch on him. Our parents don't seem to know much about the war. The sun is taking forever to slide down behind the hill. My eyelids are drooping before my soup. I prayed all afternoon, and it worked!

Now my brother is doing his homework. I watch him out of the corner of my eye while I pretend to play. Might I catch him in some heroic act? My brother, my love.

Madame M., Ham, and Francisco de Goya

The sun sets on the dusty street. I don't want to go home. They'll ask me to wash up, do my homework, they'll take my temperature, they'll narrow their eyes at my fibs, they'll comb my hair.

I stretch out the sunset as long as possible. Maybe I can make it to bed with dirty feet, without dinner, without answering questions.

Between my parents and me there is a thin wall of workaday worries, my big brother as lightning rod, and the sunset.

The street is dusty, the neighbours are in their houses. The shadows loom long, a harbinger of happiness. Above all, avoid going home.

A thin, turbaned silhouette shifts the shadows, barely: it's Madame M., the private French tutor. She is uncategorizable, exquisite. Even her mind is upright and capitalized.

Her shadow smells like perfume you can't buy in this country, just like you can't buy a head-wrap, that brooch, those manners, her glasses, her handbag, her memories. Everything about the shadow is illusory here.

Madame M. teaches us how to waltz, and about chocolate Easter eggs, *O Christmas Tree*, the map of Europe, old-fashioned balls, punctuality, the banks of the Seine, the French language, booksellers, a magnifying glass. An Alsatian doll hangs from her lamp.

She's been assigned to the village, where she and her turban positively ooze subversion.

I jealously count my shadows again. I choose the last one and I follow. Above all, I want to avoid going home.

Madame M. continues on her way to a dilapidated house near the soup kitchen. In her bag, she has an umbrella, some ham, and an art book, *The World of Francisco Goya*.

The door opens on a tangle of cats milling around a toothless old woman. Five strident cats and a little old lady, all in black, reach out their mouths to catch the pieces of ham that Madame M. throws them. The cats are more agile. They win, once, twice, three times. Five cats and an old woman, six hungry faces. A cruel smile. Madame M. loves cats.

I'm going home.

Fitting

Standing in front of the tall, silver-backed mirror, I try out the sounds of this new language, chic and haughty. I wrap my mouth around sounds, words, and phrases that until now were completely unknown in this barbaric universe: *e*, *i*, *en*. *Allons! Bonjour! Évanescent! Je vous en prie*, I beg your pardon. *La Seine a de la chance*, as the Jacques Prévert song goes. *Elle n'a pas de souci, elle se la coule douce le jour comme la nuit*. Lucky the Seine; it's all smooth sailing.

My cheeks hurt. My lips hurt, twisted around words they're not used to.

I stand up in front of the mirror and I stare at my reflection, almost to the point of tears. Who will you be, how will you be? Occasionally I talk to myself more formally. I don't want to fall into undue familiarity with someone whose destiny I don't even know.

I peer at my image as objectively as I can and try my best to guess, to predict. There are people who can read the future in the dried coffee grounds at the bottom of dainty cups. Coffee brewed and drunk, and deliberately spilled, in the name of divination.

The neighbour with the emaciated face moonlights as an oracle. She's a bit of a whore, and an unrepentant smoker. According to the old ladies, she wears bright white knickers, an unmistakable sign of her decline. She has dozens of pairs. Along with the Russians who went to Czechoslovakia and Imelda Marcos's shoe collection, it's one of the most scandalous things I've ever heard... and all the other stuff was on the radio! I run out into the gathering dusk to count the number of panties on the Pythian clothesline. There are twenty-three, all white.

I am unsettled and abashed, clambering into her chiffonier through the garden like that.

For a little money, food, or cigarettes, she predicts the future from playing cards or coffee grounds, or reads palms. For a little money, too, it is said that she will relieve men of their loneliness.

I grab a jar of honey from home and knock on

her door. She has been called a whore, a seer, and a witch for so long that her name has been forgotten. I call her Madame and I slide in as soon as she opens the door. I carefully avoid touching the handle. There are rumours, after all. The underwear! That sort of people!

I've never seen her up close and my heart is pounding. I clutch the honey. Where there is honey, nothing bad can happen. I squeeze the jar so tight my knuckles turn white and my fingers go numb.

The witch asks me to sit down. Studies in Paris? A writer? A lover? She knows the family a little bit, and I go to school with her nieces. We're all a little afraid of the nieces and we try to buy their good grace with apples or sweets.

My cheeks are burning, my ears are ringing, and my eyes are blurry. She offers me coffee, and I feel myself getting older. It's the first time I've ever been offered coffee. We turn the cup over and wait a few minutes. The witch sees a lot of joy and a lot of unhappiness, heartbreak, children, death, travel—all at the bottom of a little cup. The room grows stifling and thick scrolls of cigarette smoke blind me completely.

Fortunately, all I have to do to get out of there is push the door.

★

On the way to the church, my parents walk out in front, arm in arm, and we children follow obediently.

Every Saturday I'm jealous of the curve of my mother's legs, her dancer's ankles, delicate, tanned, and eloquent. Every Saturday, she wears her black shoes, in matte and patent leather.

The buckle at the tip of the shoes drives me crazy, to the outer limits of shoe craving. I'm actually shaking.

The shoes are antelope leather. Antelope! I gargle with this word for an animal that's not real because I've never seen one. Only once, actually, at school, in grade four, on a poorly printed picture in our geography textbook. I choke on this strange word for my mother's shoes, her Saturday shoes. The heels rock back and forth in my throat.

Ant-elope. An-te-lope.

I can't breathe! My mother's shoes stick in my craw.

Women's shoes, for women from the land of womanness. Antelope. Antelope! My father likes the straight heel and the shank, the little-girl sockettes, he praises the cobbler and the priest who tend regularly to the sole and the soul. As for me, it's no use kicking every ridge and stone in the road, I can scratch up my shoes all I want or soak them through, stomp through puddles. My shoes are solid and polished, and they'll be fixed again before the start of the school year.

I am mad with envy: the antelope, the curves, the ankles, the high heels, the stockings. I've never had high heels, not even a little high, I've never had anything like those diaphanous, fragile pantyhose, so feminine.

In front of the full-length mirror in our parents' bedroom, I yank the drawers open. There's no one at home, the sun sifts lazily through the windows. I draw the shades and I pull on my mother's pantyhose. My hands are shaking as I tug, as I breathe them in. I knew it. They smell like woman.

All I have to do to get out of my parents' room is push the door.

Mystique

I'm thirsty. I wake up in the guest bed in the living room. The long-dead clock looks like it's sticking its tongue out at me. A crystal chandelier hangs from the ceiling, an heirloom from my grandmother, her days in the city, winsome girl dressed in velvet.

The chandelier looks out of place in our stucco house. The narrow windows have iron bars painted blue, and pots of basil and scarlet geraniums skirt the edge of the house.

The village is deserted in the dry heat of summer. A dizzy fly whirrs in an empty carafe. Outside, a few crickets chirp in answer, the fly and the crickets inflecting the silence. The ants are out in the fields.

The youth have gone to the city to study, to get married, to leave behind the dirt road. The elderly are bedridden, hidden in backyards or in the cemetery. Only a few dogs stand around, in the shade, in the coolest corners.

The silence is broken by the crowing of a crazy rooster far away. Rooster, fly, cricket.

I'm thirsty. I have to get up. I glance up one last time at the chandelier fringed in crystal prisms and I drop my feet to the ground.

There's not a drop of water in the bucket. Nothing in the carafe either. I don't remember being this thirsty since I had the mumps.

My head was so swollen then, all under my ears. It hurt, a lot! And I was so thirsty, lying there in bed doing nothing, watching shapes materialize from cracks in the whitewashed ceiling. They had isolated me while I was sick so that my father and brother wouldn't catch it; apparently the mumps makes boys sterile. My mother said so, she said she heard it from the paediatrician.

When I had the mumps, my mother would come to me three or four times a day and bring me something to drink. She pressed warm oil compresses to my neck and chest.

To make me feel better, they gave me a square tin of cookies and two children's books, with words on the left and pictures on the right.

I didn't know how to read. This thirst reminds

me of that despair of being alone, in pain and unable to read the left-hand pages by sheer will.

I look in the cupboard, I scratch my head. My hair, damp and messy, tickles my neck and my ears.

The walnut wardrobe smells good, a whiff of lavender, of tobacco and mothballs. There's a man's jacket, skeins of wool, fabric scraps. It smells musty too, like beeswax and leather. A button box, belts, shoes, a lace collar, a hat.

I'm thirsty! On the top left, on a hanger, there's a wedding dress, its white lace a bit yellowed.

I slip on the wedding dress carefully over my nightgown. I look at myself in the clock glass. Very nice! The house creaks, the church bell tolls eleven. I'm nine years old, I already know that you shouldn't wear a wedding dress before your wedding, especially not a dead woman's wedding dress. It's bad luck, and you risk not getting married yourself.

I haul open the door to the sun-bleached courtyard.

My aunt showed me how to draw water. I just have to cross the path. The well is cold to the touch. A crank wheel drags up the wooden bucket.

As soon as I wrest out the piece of wood that

acts as a brake, the chain unwinds at full speed, and the bucket crashes on the surface of the water. My arms aren't strong enough, and the crank slips from my hands and whacks me in the head.

Where is everybody?

All I have to do is raise the bucket, set it on the edge of the well, and put the piece of wood back in place.

Hanging on a small chain from a curved nail is a tin cup, the cup from which the whole village drinks, even travellers. I drink from the same cup too.

The road is dusty, and empty as far as the eye can see. Where are all the people?

Dressed in my wedding gown, I walk around majestically in the dry air. A bridal procession forms quite naturally around me: the bride, a few cats curious about this apparition, two belligerent ganders asserting the whiter whiteness of their geese, bees and ladybugs drawn to the flowers in my hair.

At the very end of the dirt road there's a small hill. Little girl in a wedding dress, I walk straight ahead. I'm thirsty and I'm hot, but I don't dare scratch my head because of the dress, and the bees. I hold up the dress so I don't get it too dirty and I walk with my head tilted. Suddenly there is a freshness in the air, a breeze, a gentle whisper; the light changes.

I lift my head. Straight ahead, a vision. An extraordinary tree, leaves and sky. In that instant, I know I have seen my destiny. *God?* I whisper.

Uncle Sasha

We're in the countryside. We've eaten so well, as we always do here. Uncle Sasha raises chickens, rabbits, cattle, sheep, and turkeys.

During the holidays, in the winter and summer, we eat so well.

My uncle grows vines, gooseberries, he grows stories, and sour cherries and plums and, he swears, black tulips. We children press our eyes closed tight in front of the tulips to prove him right and, from belief and wanting, we see them turn purple, indigo, and yes, almost black.

Uncle Sasha had a copper still made for his plum brandy. He sells it on the black market, and he's never been caught. Brandy is a rare commodity these days, useful to bribe the police, or pay the doctor or even the priest. The teacher wants some. Aunt Agathe, who does our washing, wants some, too, for her rheumatism, she says, though the country is hardly drafty; the borders are well sealed. The border guards drink brandy, too, and it makes their judgement light and their hands shaky.

Stills are illegal, and their owners theoretically face jail time, but so many people in the country have rheumatism. And everyone wants to forget, so even those who don't drink alcohol keep a bottle as a talisman against what harms may come.

The brandy is also used for cupping, under the warmed glass suctioned to the skin. Some alcohol is supposed to seep into the body of the patient who's sick with a cold. And since cold sufferers want to forget too...

He lives in a small village on the edge of a stream, surrounded by hills, dusty roads, and houses that seem to fade into each other. It's far from the capital, and the farther from the capital you are, the better off you are.

Uncle Sasha loves the chickens, and he loves us children too. Strangely, though, he never looks us straight in the eye.

My mother says he is ashamed of his scarred lip, which was sliced by a doctor's scalpel.

My father says nothing.

Grandmother speaks in an odd way, with

made-up words, but we understand the language of sugar. We understand everything right away when she gives us village biscuits with *rahat*—Turkish delight—and rock candy.*

We understand the two kinds of sweets—milk and mints, which Grandmother digs out of the pockets of her apron. She always wears an apron over two or three skirts, one on top of the other. She smells worse and worse. I was spying on her once and I saw her pee standing up, dust swirling around her bare ankles. Since that day, I always only look above her waist, at the colourful gape of her apron pockets.

My mother says, *Be polite to Uncle! Be polite to your grandmother!*

My father says nothing.

And they leave the two of us there on a cheap holiday, room and board. Our aunt is never very far away.

---

* Turkish delight is soft and elastic. The small cubes taste like honey and rose water. This delicacy, *rahat-lokum*, was brought to us by the Turks. When the Ottoman Empire fell, they left it behind, just as they forgot the moussaka, the *sarmale*, the *chiftele*, and, most of all, the coffee, Turkish coffee. Rock candy, meanwhile, is used in making plum brandy. The large sugar crystals cluster along a string, like a rosary. If you lick a crystal, it breaks into smaller fragments that reflect the light.

When she's drunk, Grandmother says that Uncle Sasha buggers the animals. She swears at him, curses him, and shakes her blue iron cane over the fence.

My mother says nothing. My father says nothing.

My aunt says nothing. She makes the sign of the cross.

Uncle Sasha doesn't say anything either. He talks to the rabbits, the chickens, the still, and the pigs.

We eat very well. The country air and my uncle's cold cuts work wonders. And we don't know what bugger means. We imagine metaphorical things. We don't understand everything Grandmother says, especially when she's drunk. It must be the dialect. We decide that buggery must be a matter of dialect.

Uncle never looks us in the eye. We look at photos of him as a young man, from the time when his eyes and lips were intact.

From time to time he sings in Russian and talks about the blue roses on the Baltic Sea, Laika the dog, and Yuri Gagarin. His version of America.

The aunt smells good, and she stands guard. We always sleep in her bed, against the whitewashed wall. The lime used on the walls is apparently antiseptic. It gives the room a pleasing bluish white tinge.

For years we eat so well, away from the city and its dangers. What's that saying, about how the countryside shapes wholesome youth? Or is that travelling? In any event, since our father never says anything…

Grandmother dies. When we get back from the cemetery, her blue iron cane seems out of place leaning against the wall of the house. We feel a presence, and turmoil, as if we had forgotten to bury part of the grandmother. No one wants her blue cane.

After the burial, Uncle Sasha throws a big feast and invites the whole village. During the three days the body is laid out on the living room table, he works, cooking the best dishes to soothe the soul of the deceased. Everyone knows that after death the soul rests for forty days in the oil lamp, near the icon. There's brandy and good wine, and laughter late into the night, until the revellers head home. Everyone agrees: they've never eaten so well in all their lives.

Grandfather cries and says nothing.

My mother cries and says, *Mama!*

The aunt cries, crosses herself, and says, *Mama!*

My father says, *May she rest in peace.*

Uncle Sasha passes around short glasses and says nothing.

We children glance at the blue iron cane. We turn our backs to it and rummage through the pockets of the crumpled apron, feeling for strings of rock candy in the pockets.

Uncle Sasha says nothing more. He's gone to fetch water, gone to the river.

A Cemetery for Bees

The apple trees stand in a row from the street to the back of the garden, in full bloom. Alongside, the beehives form a fragrant, buzzing border.

Where our fence meets our neighbour's, tucked away, is a damp, shady spot. That's where, every summer during the holidays, I make a cemetery for my bees.

I often find them on the ground, dead from exhaustion during the fierce days of the harvest. Their bodies lie there, feet outstretched, eyes closed, their stingers harmless.

I place chamomile flowers next to the bees, one per grave, and I make little matchstick crosses.

In the corners of the cemetery I plant clover. Three leaves only, there's no luck for my bees. I stand back to admire my handiwork. It's beautiful; the aesthetics of mourning. I have my back to the yard, completely absorbed by my secret avocation. I even filched a teaspoon to use as a spade to dig the tiny graves.

I find ants, too, red and black ants, and ants that died while carrying an egg. The dead ones look like they're already mummified, they've already turned to dust.

The rarest ones have translucent white wings, longer than their bodies, like wedding veils turned into shrouds. Winged ants are an anomaly I don't understand.

My brother plays with matches too, but not to make crosses. He's a pyromaniac. I read about it in his history book, a man named Nero. My brother sets all kinds of things on fire. Of what he burns, I like the rockets best, made of aluminum foil and loaded with the torn-off teeth of plastic combs. His launch pads are fashioned from wooden clothes pegs.

We line them up five or six in a row on the tin roofs of the hives, and then we light them on fire. It's very exciting. We scare ourselves a little just before we strike the match. There's smoke everywhere, and stray sparks singe our hands and hair. The charred, paltry remnants of our liftoffs lie in the grass around the hives.

Our summer holidays cost our parents a lot of

money for matches, combs, and clothes pegs.

I often return to my corner graveyard during the day. Sometimes I bury a dragonfly, and once I come across a beetle.

But the beetle looks too pretty, and I don't want to bury it. Instead, I build a shrine—a cross, a little white flower, another cross, another chamomile flower, a cross, the beetle, another cross, more chamomile. The result is stunning.

Each year, at the beginning of the summer holidays, I have to start it all over again, the cemetery for bees.

Ecumenicum

It starts to rain, warm, fat drops. The neighbour children come crying.

There are three of them, two girls and a boy.

The older sister, Teresa, is holding her little black dog in her arms. The dog is dead, but still warm. You can see a piece of pink tongue hanging out.

All the parents are at work, and their grandmother is deaf, so we're left to come up with a funeral by ourselves.

The boy, Victor, is looking for a shovel so he can dig a real grave, out at the far end of the courtyard, where we tore three planks out of the fence to get from one garden to the other more quickly. Our furtive games happen beyond our parents' watchful gaze, and at a different pace.

A kitchen towel will have to do in lieu of a

shroud, and a medallion with a cross for my little Catholic neighbours. They also found candle stumps, and we light them.

As for me, a tie of my father's and his Bible under my arm give me the air I imagine a Protestant minister officiating at a funeral should have.

We sit on the ground and place the body of the dog in the grave. We have to talk doctrine, too—a dog must have an immortal soul, more than a cat or a bee but less than a person. My neighbours are adamant that in church you answer the priest from your soul.

The youngest among us, Antoinetta, is always whining, and when we talk about souls she starts to cry harder. Now she's not sure anymore that the dog has a soul. She's such a dummy.

Last year, when I buried my doll beneath the walnut tree, she believed me right away when I told her my doll had a soul. I'm seized by a terrible thought: had she been thinking that day of robbing the grave? I'd never even seen her with a doll. Last year, along with the other children, Antoinetta ate the cakes and sweets I set out in memory of the doll. History tells us that sweets and shiny things have a lot to do with converting the heathens.

We begin the funeral service. The other children make the sign of the cross, while I hold the Bible tight, *sola scriptura*. My father told me that making the sign of the cross is like making the sign of the electric chair, an acknowledgment of how we put people to death. And in fact, I tried in private to make up a sign of the electric chair, succeeding, I think, kind of. In Jesus's time, electricity hadn't been discovered, and so judges and soldiers used to put the condemned on a cross and leave them there to die of hunger and thirst. A spear was thrust into the heart to confirm death.

What if the dog isn't really dead? What if the dog is only asleep?

We stop everything and we sit down again in the grass. I'm not willing to bite the dog's paw to check, I tell them, so we need a mirror. Antoinetta, happy to be assigned such an important task, stops whining and goes to get a mirror from the house. It's a perilous mission; the grandmother may be deaf, but she can see everything.

We wait a little, the mirror arrives, and we hold it in front of the dog's nose. We think we see mist and movement, but it's just our own uneven breathing, our sweaty hands, the wind. He looks fairly dead, very dead even. A few flies and some curious bees are swirling around in the increasingly warm air.

The candles have melted down, and we proceed to the burial. We're all hungry, and animated by a sense of urgency. We've been gravediggers for too long already.

I sing a hymn of hope and resurrection, and we all recite the Lord's Prayer together at full speed. To finish things off, we place two small branches in the shape of a cross over the fresh grave.

Each week, our parents continue to bring us to our respective services, with some respite at Christmas and Easter when we also go to the other churches a few times, to be neighbourly. Over the fence, the parents exchange Easter cakes, eggs dyed red, willow branches on Palm Sunday, and lamb and bitter herbs.

The real fence, the official adult fence, the one you see from the street, bears a small enamelled plaque with the number 63 written in blue and white.

Casting

On the train that whisks us away on vacation, we sit, father, mother, brother, sister. I keep checking my wrist to make sure my watch is still there. It's a small, round watch, gold-plated, with a light grey patent-leather strap. I have never seen such a beautiful watch. It was a gift from my parents for my first prize honours at the end of the school year. My father calls me his little student of letters.

The other travellers seem to be having a lot of fun, especially a group of doctors in particle physics.

The leather of the first-class booths smells faintly like cigarettes. In the seat across from ours, a slightly drunk student tells us how he lost a bet with friends and had to eat eight hard-boiled eggs. He gives us chocolate, and we play cards.

I find him attractive, and I am happy to have a wristwatch like a real lady. My brother and I decided to call the student Eight Eggs and make him our friend. He is going to the same seaside resort we are for two weeks. From now on, we travel together, father, mother, brother, sister. Our parents are relaxed, they let us do what we want, draped in their holiday magnanimity.

It's a long ride, and the dull clacking of the wheels makes the passengers drowsy. I dream troubled dreams and wake up with a start, thirsty. The bump on the middle finger of my right hand is throbbing. It's a writer's bump, blue with ink. They say that a hunchback's hump is good luck. My finger is hunchbacked because I squeeze my pen too hard. I want so, so badly to trace perfect letters. My notebooks are often stained with ink, and for some reason the glass ink bottle I carry in my school bag started to leak. I cried a lot this year, I had to rewrite a lot of my homework. I wanted that first prize honours. The winner gets a crown, a wreath made of oak leaves with rosebuds all around, and books as gifts—three for first prize, two for second, and one for the third prize winner. The honourable mentions get no book at all, just a pointless certificate.

As I looked at the titles I'd won, holding my

head very straight so I wouldn't drop the crown, I thought I had lost out. One of the books was called *Fish in the Trees*, the second was *Pepper Caramels*. I thought they were making fun of me, though my pulse still throbbed in the bump on my finger. Fortunately, the third book was called *Legends of Olympus*.

I feel my wrist. At least I got the watch from my parents—a sure value. And it's my birthday in two days. I will be eight years old.

The train whistles. We've arrived at our destination, and we are all ravenous.

My brother has a girlfriend I'm interested in, but the student is interested in her too, so my brother and I decide that he will no longer be our friend. We would much rather have the girlfriend, who's a head taller than my brother, blonde, and has a suitcase full of jars and multivitamins. My favourite is the chewable vitamin C, which I eat with white bread. The vitamin girlfriend also has chocolate and sugar and cocoa powder. In her room, when our parents aren't around, we make cones out of paper and mix sugar and cocoa and we suck and lick the mixture through a hole in the base of the cone. We keep choking on it. The fine cocoa powder puffs away with the slightest breath and tickles our throats, deliciously.

In the afternoon, we take a family walk in the park, mother, father, brother, sister. It means a lot to my father.

Everything unfolds as it should, each of us playing our part. The little girl acts like a little girl, leaving the grown-ups to fend for themselves, as usual. She looks around now and then to find out what they expect of her and to watch for the right moment to say her line.

Inventory: the hair neatly braided, the unwavering smile, the socks pulled tight.

The mother, who no longer has to cook, plays the role of a mother on vacation, reading and knitting. As a holiday activity, she also gossips with the other wives she meets in restaurants or along the paths of the city's only park. The big brother plays the big brother, avoiding the father as much he can, and the father plays a father on vacation, though not yet a happy father. On the other hand, he does start buying ice cream cones, a break from his frugal habits, and a sign of exceptional inner torment, because do real fathers buy ice cream?

You have to stick to your part. The father wants to. Late in the evening, after a band concert in the park's ornate wooden gazebo, the hotel doors close on the families on holiday. Our rooms are on the second floor.

But just before we fall asleep, a low rumble below us makes the whole floor vibrate, startling everybody. Our father scrambles down the back stairs in his pyjamas and finds himself among a group of men, about twenty of them, also in their pyjamas, huddled in front of a radio at the hotel reception desk. The women, in their night-dresses, stay in the rooms, waiting for the men to return with news. Nobody is paying any attention to the children.

At this non-such hour, grown-up hour, I'm astonished as I watch the gathering of gentlemen in pyjamas, my father too. They are all dressed identically, and they listen to the radio in identical silence.

The Radio Europa Libera broadcasts the report: the Russians are in Prague. The pyjamas discuss the likely consequences of this extraordinary news. We'll be next! Should we stay put or go straight home? Go buy biscuits and preserves! Batten down the hatches!

No one pays attention to the children. The universe is broken. At this hour, the gentlemen in pyjamas, my father among them, are putting on a scandalous show.

I rub my inky bump anxiously, my right hand

hidden in the pocket of my dressing gown. If a hunchback's hump is lucky, then I wish for a return to order.

I hide in the corner of the staircase, from where I have a bird's eye view of the foyer. I pray for a return to our regular roles. But history has no blotter. The next day, at dawn, suitcases in hand, we head back home. The pyjamas have decided that we're next, it's inevitable. The women packed the bags, our holiday left unfinished. Tomorrow is my birthday. Eight years old. On the train, on the way home, it's father, mother, brother, sister, and everybody else.

The student says goodbye and leaves the coach. No one is laughing, no one speaks. What will we find at home? It's still the holidays!

I feel my wrist to make sure my wristwatch is still there. The brother sneaks a glimpse at the piece of paper with the vitamin girlfriend's address. The mother nervously takes up her knitting needles, but she keeps making mistakes and has to start again.

The father has recovered his costume and his wits, and the categories are back in place, the roles have been assigned for good.

I haven't seen another foreign man in pyjamas since. Nor my father, for that matter.

My Father's Watch and My Mother's Tapestries

Sailors are among the lucky few who can leave the country, and who can take advantage of the black market to make some money. For us, the word *navigatori* evokes wealth and travel. In Romania, sailors have beautiful houses by the Black Sea and their wives live lavish lives, taking care of the house and the children, on condition that they sit and wait, white widows, for the return of their husbands, who sail around the world for six months at a time, or even a year.

The sailors sell *blugi*—blue jeans—and vitamins, watches, comic books. My father bought an Atlantic brand wristwatch from them. The dial is midnight blue and the hands are gold. All the watches I've seen before were white; this dark blue seems rebellious to me, charged with a mysterious, seditious meaning. It's a tunnel that can let us cross beneath the border, travel abroad, unseen and unknown.

I dream of escape, I am twelve years old.

The *navigatori* also sell wedding dresses, just like in Paris they say, and coffee, and allegedly Persian carpets.

My mother has two tapestries, nailed to the bedroom walls. The first one represents *The Abduction of the Sabine Women*. The Sabines are wearing period clothing, and they are not at all shy. The second tapestry, *Night in Venice*, is a woven cliché, with a gondolier's straw boater in the foreground. In the background, masked couples are dancing and flirting, or at least that's what their props seem to suggest, the costumes and domino masks, the mandolins, the fans.

I've spent hours of my childhood contemplating these shocking, sensual images. You can't always control what comes through customs. I heard my mother tell a neighbour that she actually ordered a reproduction of *The Last Supper*.

She had to keep up, so she took what she got.

Time passes, and the tapestries become part of the household, sometimes hilariously. *I refreshed the* Sabines, my mother will say, *I aired out the* Night in Venice or, even better, *the lagoon is getting munched by moths.*

I don't even want to think how Jesus and the apostles would have fared.

The tapestries' silk fringes grow bald as a result of our childhood games. We knot the threads and then gently pull them out. I like the feel of the silk slipping, and of doing something illicit, the thrill of anticipated punishment. The thrill, too, of not being discovered. Over time, the abduction of the Sabines starts to look like an eye without lashes. Our mother, who's completely oblivious to our misdeeds, muses that they don't make tapestries like they used to.

But she's a woman of action, she doesn't fall apart. Instead, she sews sturdy wool fringes all around the tapestry. The Sabines are no longer merely dressed, they're swaddled.

The edges of the Venetian night, on the other hand, prove to be unremovable. So I sit and contemplate, I spend long hours in front of this image. *Din străinătate*: from abroad, from the outside.

The trend for hand-stitched reproductions rages on, the local women taking up the fine, tiny stitches. These designers and weavers have obviously never been to Venice, they've probably only seen postcards, which in turn were reproductions of drawings and other postcards.

After two and a half years of needlework, a caricature of a caricature of an idea of Venice covers the western wall of the bedroom.

Ours is the only house in the whole village that has two Venices.

Farm Soap

I close the door. I leave the light off. The water flows into the sink, ice cold. I pick up the big bar of farm soap. It's heavy, it's grey, and it sticks to my hands, leaving marks on the wet fabric.

My mother's blood and urine. I scrub and scrub and my fingers get colder and colder.

I'm washing out my mother's blood and urine.

My mother is drunk. She's curled up on the wool mattress, she doesn't turn on the light, doesn't speak. Like a child she squeezes her eyes shut, so hard she shudders, so hard the world turns white. She closes her eyes so that the world disappears. A prayer, make it be all just a dream, I'll count to three.

She's drunk, my mother is suffering, and this is the instant in which I begin to love her.

The cold chills me to the bone, all the way up

my arms. I rub, wash, I swallow hard and choke. My mother's blood and urine make my head spin but still I wash, scrub, rinse. The fabric tears. There is no way anyone else can be allowed to see her blood, her drunkenness; not my father, my brother, the neighbours, not even my mother herself.

Not even my mother; she couldn't stand it.

Soap sticks to the panties, to the skirt; the ice water sets the stains, imprinted on my retina and washed away.

Tomorrow morning there will be no trace of soap or inebriation. Her clothes will be folded neatly on the chair, though I should crumple them slightly, otherwise she'll notice. I wash and scrub in the damp dark.

My mother's blood and urine. Is that all it was?

A Bright Future

The headmistress of the school is always well turned out. She's a woman who gives the impression that she sleeps standing up, all dressed up and with her hair done. Her hairstyle is that stiff.

Even a single hair sticking out would have made her look approachable. Walking behind her in the hallway, the boldest students blow as hard as they can to try to make her hair move.

The headmistress strides into our classroom. *You know, children, if your parents or your neighbours say something bad about Comrade Ceaușescu, you must come and tell us. It's your duty as a Pioneer. Nothing shall stop the glorious march of the country, my children. It's marching toward your future. Your bright future.*

We are twelve years old and the school intercoms were installed just two weeks earlier—officially so that the school management can announce general interest messages. No one is fooled. The school's higher-ups and the secret police are listening to what is said in the classrooms.

Teachers and students, at attention!

In order to march to the bright future and to thwart our arch-enemies (the capitalists) and our pseudo-enemies (the other socialist countries) we must create an *omul nou*, the New Man. We must be flawless, docile, and guileless. During meetings of the Pioneer Organization, the Union of Communist Youth, the Party, we must be on the lookout. There's no need to specify the name of the party, there's only one legal political party, the Communist Party.

You also have to denounce yourself from time to time. It's called self-criticism.

Yes, comrades, I have read forbidden books, I have neglected my duties as citizen.

Yes, I have an uncle in the West. My roots are healthy otherwise, neither Jews nor gypsies, my grandparents fought in the war. I am of wholesome stock.

It's true, I go to church. Yes, my religion was imported from America. Yes, I promise to make amends.

This is the glorious era during which the Great Leader leads a confused country. He takes up the only half hour of airtime on our lone television channel. We watch him from time to time, to see if there is any news—maybe he looks a little weakened, a bit sick—or to find out sooner rather than later what other misfortune will befall us.

At night we take the transistor radio out of its drawer and get news of ourselves from stations abroad, from those who have taken advantage of Party congresses abroad to defect, and who've had to change their faces and their life stories. On Radio Europa Libera or Vocea Americii the defectors tell us what is going on in our country.

That's how we learn about Chernobyl, although we're right next door, at the border. An engineer friend brings a Geiger counter to church to measure the radiation. The tomatoes and the *telemea* are lethal, the device shows; that feta cheese has radiation levels that could have killed us a hundred times over.

Months later, in May, the state takes steps to combat radiation. Iodine pills are distributed, and as soon as rain clouds loom on the horizon, we have to stay indoors, man and beast.

New topics, new political jokes. Toothsome jokes. This is how humour delays revolutions.

For Four Hands

I've just come from school, it's spring. In front of the house, there is a moving truck, the same one we use for funerals. Today it's grey and blue, but the people at the town hall drape it in black cloth when they rent it to bereaved families. I usually see it in black, with funeral wreaths and incense. My heart is racing.

One… two! One, two!

A huge grand piano is lowered from the truck by the movers, before the amazed eyes of the neighbours, who are pressed up against the fence. The piano is my mother's acquisition. She has no ear for music, but considerable ambition for her children, and the piano's brass pedals are just the spring needed for our social advancement.

The piano is large, heavy, disproportionate. Its feet sink into the floor where the floorboards are rotten from having been painted too soon, in burgundy, by my mother.

Mother-of-pearl letters inlaid on the keyboard's domed lid read *Nemetschke & Sohn*.

For a long time I am fascinated by this intruder, an unusual creature in our familiar setting. I pretend to leave and then spin around abruptly to try to catch the piano in the act. You never know.

I point to it with my finger, show my brother. I don't dare speak. The piano echoes when we talk loudly or sing, but most of the time it remains impassive, wood and bronze, proudly imprisoned in our floor.

During the night, when I'm asleep, everything is fine, as it was before. But in the morning, when we wake up, it's still there, and in the evening at bedtime, too. We will have to get used to it.

Our mother cleans the floor and the piano every Tuesday and Thursday with blind faith. Her children will shine. She never fails to boast about her children's piano lessons when she goes to the market. The eggs she buys are more beautiful, the herbs more fragrant, the mushrooms raise their little caps smartly.

Tuesdays and Thursdays, our piano lesson days, have a special flavour now. We have to cut our nails short, wash our ears, avoid eating garlic.

We play, we get used to it. The piano is a house, a boat, a hiding place. My sweets! My coins! I kneel down, quickly slip under the piano and look for my treasures in the wooden frame.

Phew! It's all there, right where it belongs.

My brother too hides his riches in the dusty bowels of the piano. We often come across each other's stash, but we don't let on.

Mrs. Hantellman teaches us piano, and in the winter she gives orange liqueur to the children whose lessons are her livelihood. Her little pupils. For years, it is the only alcohol that crosses our lips, and our little secret.

Her house smells like lavender, coffee, and warm piano, though her instrument is a narrow upright.

In the tiny entranceway, the boots and umbrellas of the students who've just arrived are heaped together for a while with the shoes and umbrellas of the students who are leaving, that much more skilled, their cheeks bright with artistic emotion.

Mrs. Hantellman, a German Jew who stayed in the country after the war, has a unique touch and a democratic spirit; she takes money from all the parents. In exchange, they are condemned to listen to the same tune, which is rehearsed at length at home and replayed ad nauseam in front of any guests.

Even the parents of children who make no progress whatsoever acquire some light musical culture and solid provincial snobbery, albeit for a price.

Today, I hid gum in the piano; the brother hid a love note. He found my gum, chewed it a little and put it back in its wrapper. He didn't like the taste.

I found the note, read it, folded it carefully and put it back in its place; I didn't like the bland taste of the girl who had written to him either.

The grand piano... Just owning a piano! A grand piano, imagine. The longer the tail, the more devoted the children.

★

The day wanes, another Thursday, another piano lesson. The metronome is a critter stirring in the spartan setting.

One-two-three, one-two-three. My palm, held rounded over an imaginary ball, cramps up. Mrs. Hantellman's hazelnut switch reminds me to lift my wrists and, without warning, lashes my forgetful, obstinate fingers.

After a syncopated rest, the child and the metronome start up again. Faster, faster! Let's get it over with, one-two-three, one-two-three! I glare at the score and at the hazelwood rod.

My mother has no ear, but considerable ambition for her children. She knits covers for the piano bench, she buys rococo candles, and every Tuesday and Thursday she vigorously polishes the piano and the wooden floor. She paints a trompe l'œil around the holes in the floor under the piano, which is heavy and utterly disproportionate, and which aspires only to rest directly on the beaten earth.

I rehearse at length the left hand, and, despairing, the right. I rarely play both at the same time.

Arrogant and a little distracted, my father listens to my graceless efforts from a distance. He played piano as a child too, and views these lessons and exercises much as one might the obligatory illnesses of childhood. As with vaccinations, and in order not to be accused of negligence by my mother, he dutifully pays for the lessons.

Left hand, right hand. My brother plays well and without too much fuss. The pieces are carefully chosen. He plays in church, too, accompanying the congregation.

We learn "The Donkey," my brother with two

hands and me with one. It's a silly number, well known to any child who's taken piano lessons, for three hands.

The pile of piano books stares at me balefully. Czerny, Hummel, Carl Czerny opus 529, Czerny opus 841, the *Notebooks for Ana Magdalena Bach*.

One-two-three! One-two-three! The metronome stutters like castanets as the day wanes.

One-two-three! One-two-three!

I'm definitely in awe of this piano. It's big, it has its own secrets. I make offerings, baskets of apples and chrysanthemums in the fall, and in winter pears, apples, and quinces. In the spring, whole branches of lilacs, the flowering branches of apple trees.

Unaccountably, my father says nothing about my floral slaughter.

My brother grows distant. He no longer hides anything in the piano. He gets a leather wallet for his fifteenth birthday, he takes up painting.

He listens from a distance, with an absent-minded and somewhat disdainful ear. For him, piano is outdated, tedious, though he kindly brings me new scores.

The pile of scores grows higher, looking down at me reproachfully. Czerny, Hummel, Diabelli and his sonatinas, J. S. Bach, the preludes and fugues and *The Well-Tempered Clavier*.

One, two! One, two! The day wanes and the metronome acts out.

There's still not much progress on the piano front. I'm a teenager, acting out. I do feel like I owe it to my mother, to justify the purchase of the piano, all the expense, and to maintain her dazzling vision of her children, impeccable, surrounded by exquisite, well-dressed and well-educated people who all know how to play the piano. Each piano lesson strikes a new match that keeps her vision burning.

My mother knits artistic scarves, berets, and gloves. I pose, *Young Girl at the Piano, with Beret*.

Like an old husband besotted and impotent, I occasionally offer the instrument an accomplished pianist. It vibrates, it sounds, it resounds and they enjoy each other together as I watch jealously; I go around again and again, with coffee, sorbet, jam.

I grow up. Father pays for the lessons, mother scrubs the floor, and I listen to the great pianists.

The brother defiantly switches to sculpture and medicine. From time to time he brings me some sheet music or a record. From time to time, too, he brings home a girl who plays the piano. I obediently pass the coffee, the sorbet, I clean up.

Over the spring holidays he scores with a cousin over the piano lid. To each their trophy, to each their offerings.

Mrs. Hantellman no longer teaches lessons or gives children orange liqueur. She lost her husband, and her house smells like beeswax and candles. She smells too, like camphor and loneliness.

One Tuesday in spring, she comes to visit us at home and plays happily on my piano. Now it is legitimate.

From time to time, the strings go slack and the piano loses its voice, so the tuner comes to take care of it in exchange for a few good meals.

I slip under the piano and the music rolls through me, voluptuously.

★

I rehearse at length the left hand part, and, despairing, the right. I cannot play both at the same time.

The brother gets bored, packs up, and leaves the country. He takes up archaeology and hang-gliding. From time to time he sends me famous recordings, vitamins, and chocolate.

The neighbour children sit on the pile of music, as if that's what it's for. Their feet don't touch the ground. And they play wonderfully well, by ear. There are five of them, dirty and a bit wild, but they all play like gods. They ask for food.

★

A few years later, in the evening, I've just come back from a trip, it's fall. In front of the house, the moving truck, the same one they use for funerals. My heart races. One… two! And one… two!

I put my suitcase down. This time there are no curious neighbours at the fence. They're sleeping, they're dead, they've seen it all.

With a final effort, the movers hoist the grand piano into the truck. The piano has been sold by the mother with no ear for music. Everything is there, the copper pedals, burnished with some of the blood-coloured paint from the floor, the bench, my childhood, the scores, the holes in the floor, my mother's tin ear, the social aspirations, the candles, the gloves and beret.

Byzantine

DRESS REHEARSAL

Subtitles

The border checkpoint is buried under snow. In the train car the air is getting colder and colder. Mists of breath mingle in the requisite silence while the benches and ceilings, dismantled by soldiers, spill their innards. They say someone tried to hide something in there to sell it to the Russians. In the silence, buttocks squeeze together over rolls of paper rubles slipped into the fingers of surgical gloves. They say someone tried to sneak across the border, that he died. Or she died. Or two people died, there are many rumours.

Terrified travellers are waiting to be searched, even the elderly, even children, even the sick, even pregnant women. They say that last time...

★

Elsewhere in the geography book, skin goes brown, pass the sugar, smells change. Eyes darken and narrow like they do in the act of love.

At the border, which is open on one side only, opened by the treason of even just a single person, bare breasts push the eastern limit of desire. Without papers, they prostitute themselves at the border.

Word of mouth gets chatty.

Between the evening paper and suppertime, Eastern European girls stretch out across full-page spreads, tickle the West's yearning for exoticism. In Kundera's satchel, they fade, defecting from their language, worn out by each successive translation.

Kundera started translating himself for the La Pléiade library collection, he changed his jacket and wore his most elegant tie.

What is it that makes them all want to shut themselves up in the Pleiades?

★

On the outside, they say, you can buy anything you want, the stalls are overflowing with food, everyone has a car. In the West, you can stand in the middle of the street and shout, *Down with So-*

and-so.

Hush, they can hear us. At the border open on one side only, made porous by the treason of a single person, bare breasts are pushing at the door. They say that in Amsterdam hookers swim in shop windows.

In the requisite silence, the mist gets chatty. They say that in Paris, Brâncuși lived all his life in a dead end after coming kiss to kiss with Rodin. He had no money, so he walked all the way there. Once he'd arrived, he set up his studio and shuffled off. They transferred the workshop to the Pompidou and his remains to the Montparnasse cemetery.

What is it that makes them all want to be entombed at Père-Lachaise or Montparnasse?

★

A lady who has travelled tells us that on the outside, during a Communist Youth conference, she was able to get powdered milk, Bayer aspirin, chocolate, and coffee. No one had to stand in line. Yet after this glimpse of heaven she still returned home. She couldn't abandon her graves.

We squeeze our buttocks to make sure the rubles are still there. On the journey home, gold is best hidden in toothpaste tubes. You undo the bottom of the tube, remove a reasonable amount of toothpaste, tuck in your gold rings, roll up the bottom of the tube so that the gold is rolled up too, and then dent the tube slightly. With a bit of luck, the metal detectors at customs will let it through. Back in the country, where wedding rings are officially sold mainly to deserving workers, you can run a brisk business. Lovers want to get married. Since no girl wants to get married without a wedding ring, they're willing to pay.

At the border, which is open on one side only, Ionesco, as a diversion, releases his rhinos and they trample the earth furiously. Once he arrives safe and sound on the other side, he begins to write in absurd French and to roll his *r*s. The immortals at the Académie française, thrown off by this upstart with the nerve to lecture them, offer him a chair, number six. For the occasion Ionesco has to don an embroidered suit, comb his *r*s, clean his glasses, and pay homage to the man who gave up his chair. Shortly afterwards he also moves to the Montparnasse, where he turns over in his grave every time he remembers that the other guy is there too for his eternal rest, waiting for Godot.

What is it that makes them all want to sit in the Académie and have their plays staged at the

Théâtre de la Huchette?

★

In the history textbook, at the eastern limit of desire, Georges Enescu crosses the border, with his feisty bow and his rabbit's-fur muff, violin tucked under his arm and passport in hand.

He leaves Lipatti at home, leaves him for dead and heads for the applause, for an unattainable love, for French papers.

After a detour in America, Enescu rushes on to Père-Lachaise, exhausted by concerts and wars, against the backdrop of his childhood in Moldavia and the stone-ground landscape.

His *Romanian Rhapsody* draws some people back to the country, further weakening the border. Treason in reverse.

On scholarship at the conservatory, for his first scratch at posterity, Georges Enescu is master, sir, maestro, a child prodigy, genius, one of a kind, big news in the music world. His violins are sold, scholarships are created in his name, they try to repatriate his body.

When he was little, at home, his parents called him Jurjac.

Coffee at the Embassy

I'm called to come in for an interview at the Canadian Embassy in Bucharest.

Spring is here! After the lilies of the valley and the lilacs, passport season is approaching. Cherry season, too.

I'm dressed in an outfit for the West, like those who buy on credit and spend against their next paycheque, dressed on a borrowed dime. I spend a sleepless night on the train, nine hours. I am being watched, my elegance is out of place on the night train.

Travelling at night means I don't have to be apart from my child for too long, and I will arrive on time when the embassy opens. As is customary, I have a packet of coffee in my travel bag. Anyone can be coaxed, made more charitable.

A cordon of Romanian soldiers, showily

armed, stands by the lineup in the street outside the embassy.

They search our bags, find my coffee. *What is this for,* doamna*?*

Doamna? No more *comrade*. I already feel singled out. My ears are ringing.

I bought some coffee for myself, to drink. The first rule of survival is never tell the truth—or rather, tell the truth, but tell it slant.

Come now, doamna*!* The corners of the coffee bag are worn, it's already been passed around. The Romanian soldiers at the embassy have special training but they live in this country too, they know. Doamna*, we would look like fools in front of the Canadians*.

Shame? How delightful! Can there be such a thing as the rule of law? I feel like I've stepped onto Western soil. The coffee confiscated by the soldier before my meeting is returned to me. The soldier apparently doesn't take bribes either. Back on the train, five hours this time, it's the *tren accelerat*, I am rich in coffee not given, redundant coffee, *the embassy employees get a salary,* doamna. My whole understanding of the world is turned upside down and suddenly I imagine a wealth of possibilities.

Once I get home, I give the coffee back to my

mother. She opens the packet and roasts the beans for a few minutes in the oven, sprinkling them with rum.

She grinds the coffee, fills an *ibrik** with water, spoons in the coffee and sugar. She takes the small cups out of the china cabinet, the special occasion cups, guest cups.

We pour hot, fragrant, sweet coffee. And we start laughing: *Mama, we've having coffee at the embassy!*

---

* The *ibrik* is a coffee pot used to prepare Turkish or Greek coffee, or, for purists, espresso. To brew the best coffee in the world, you will need two heaping teaspoons of ground coffee and one teaspoon of sugar per cup of water. When the water boils, remove the *ibrik* from the heat and add the coffee, which will froth. Hold the pot over the flame, without putting it down. As for the artful details, let the *ibrik* stand for two or three minutes so that the coffee grounds settle to the bottom. Pour into tiny, pretty cups. Drink it in small sips. And finally, the clairvoyant aftertaste: turn the cups over and prophesy the future—weather and financial forecasts, weddings, betrayals, deaths, sometimes even wars. The moral is that, without this adumbrative beverage, those on a coffeeless diet never knew the Wall would come down.

The Button Box

Since the people around me found out that I am going to leave the country, they treat me with the deference and aloofness reserved for those who are no longer quite there anymore, like the terminally ill.

I want them to treat me like a living person, like I still belong. With the idea of departure, a veil of light flicks before my eyes for the first time.

While I'm in Bucharest to pick up the passport, my mother takes it upon herself to launch into some spring cleaning. She digs up and moves my white lilac. When I return, my room is very clean, just two unpacked suitcases, undecided and forever unready.

My mother has already buried me. Mourning in reverse. I am inconsolable.

With the passport in my pocket, the first one

I've ever had, I set out on my farewell tour. Instead of bringing flowers, I show the passport to those who've never seen one before. I am twenty-eight years old, the child is almost three.

I also go see the family of an officer in the Securitate, our persecutors. To my surprise, the father tells me not to forget our country, and to do it honour when I am abroad. I do not show him the passport. Their son is a childhood friend.

As in every house I visit, I ask if I can look in their button box. The button boxes contain real gems.

First of all, there's the box itself, often an old candy box, a metal tin, or a halva box with red and gold stripes.

But it's what's in the box—single earrings, antique buttons, modern buttons, jewellery that's lost a stone and looks cockeyed, *mărțișor* of yore.

Mărțișor—the word means little March—are small plastic or metal baubles hung on a white and red thread. They're given as gifts every year on March first to celebrate the coming of spring. Women, men, and children wear them pinned to their coat lapels throughout the month of March.

Of all the goodies in button boxes, my favourite finds are the medals and badges from when we were Pioneers, between the ages of ten and fourteen. After that you had to join the Communist Youth.

Some of my friends had shoulders and shirt-fronts full of these pins and ribbons, real little generals, gold medallists for discipline, for having planted the most trees, for having earned tens during a whole school year, for having won first prize in regional or national math, literature, or chemistry competitions, for having been first in sports, for excellent results in the pre-military training camp.

I was the standard bearer of our *Pionierii* detachment and I took my job to heart. Never had the flag been washed and ironed as often as during my tenure.

In pre-military training I was platoon commander. I dislocated my shoulder during firing exercises, and the others hated me because I tried too hard. I took it all very seriously. I was ready to defend my country. In our collective imagination, the Russians had been at our doorstep since they had entered Czechoslovakia. And, to tell the truth, only a few kilometres, a few orders separated the feared and the real.

I knew the language of authority, I had studied Russian for four years in high school. I had chosen English, while Russian was imposed.

It's no surprise; since the end of World War II, Romanians have been waiting for the Americans, but the only ones who've come have been the Russians. They even wanted to come back in 1968. After the invasion of Czechoslovakia, the Russian threat was Ceaușescu's moment of glory. He called for independence and political sovereignty, for non-intervention in our domestic affairs.

The West made him a hero, and an ally against the Soviets, but for the people, within our closed borders, there was no conceivable salvation. At first, nationalism made him a hero too. After that there were no limits to the tyranny, no obstacles.

At the pre-military training camp, boys and girls lived in separate quarters. To avoid amorous encounters, our morning tea was laced with sleeping powder—without our knowledge, of course. The language of love and the language of authority, night and day.

A slightly oily film on the surface of the tea betrayed the presence of the potassium bromide. Based on information from my brother, who had already done his military service and who had drunk many a cup of bromide-flavoured tea, I made my reputation spreading the conspiracy of the tea to the others. I also organized a dance party.

Never had a training uniform been washed and ironed or military boots shined as brightly as during my pre-military summer camp.

I was fourteen years old. I brought my Union of Communist Youth Diploma of Merit to school. My father had paid to have it framed, and the headmistress hung it on the wall in the corridor near the teachers' lounge.

I slip the diploma in the dictionary, hide the merit badges among my jewellery, and the souvenir buttons in the makeup bag. One more go at arranging the suitcase. What should I take, what should I leave with my parents?

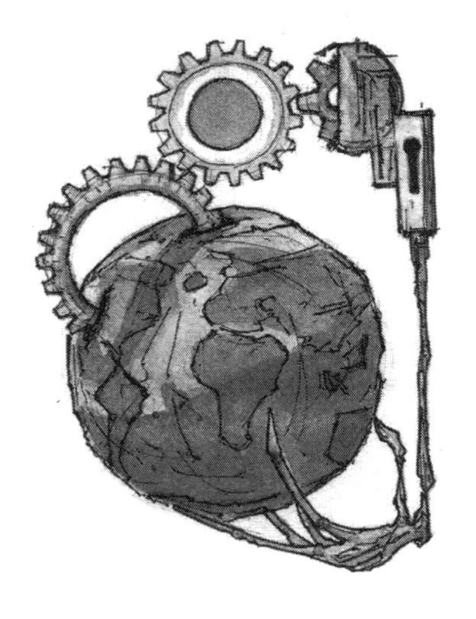

The turning world

GENESIS (APOCRYPHON)

The First Day

As always, while I sleep, those in the know wind the wheels of the world.

The world turns, and the world changes. They ride along, set things in motion, dismantle what needs dismantling, redraw the borders.

With steel wrenches and heavy feet.

They know about factories, and hospitals, they know the distance between the Earth and the Moon, the recipe for bread.

They know how to wash the dead, sew clothes, develop vaccines, and isolate radioactive isotopes.

Those in the know are exemplars, they make people believe, they keep up appearances.

I wonder in what language they give orders. Is there one language for day and another for night?

I stretch out and I remember. Last night I landed at Mirabel, Montreal's international airport.

With two suitcases, and also with the child.

My brother, who has been here for two years already, wrote to me that they never wait in line to buy food and that Canada rests on a shield, a tectonic plate, so there are no earthquakes. And at the airport, right away, he also warned me, *Above all, don't speak France French, they'll hate you!* He said it in Romanian, obviously.

No earthquakes, don't sound like you're French, but there's bread, eggs, milk, bananas, apples, oil... and perfume, one day, when I have money.

In Romania, everyone my age has a traumatic memory of March 4, 1977, when a huge earthquake, 7.2 on the Richter scale, shook the Eastern Carpathians, a region located at the junction of several particularly active tectonic microplates. Since then, the phrase tectonic plate, with its solemn Teutonic consonance, has made me tremble.

Part of the historic centre of Bucharest was destroyed. In its place, for months and months, stood an esplanade of dread and death.

The cloying smell of decomposing bodies is impossible to forget.

Famous people, actors, musicians, writers lost their lives. Eviscerated churches laid bare their Holy of Holies, and all kinds of objects of worship were stolen.

The saints had been warned in time, at dawn, and had fled through the window.

Inside information.

They were perpetual saints. I don't know what they'd been accused of, but they must have had enough of arches and incense.

They were in such a hurry that they left naked, forgetting their halos.

Even just the day before, there they were, upright, unmoving and unsmiling. They were all at the table. The one in the middle was apparently a bastard, father unknown. To fit in, he made up stories and ways of the cross, parables; he even passed himself off as the son of God. There were twelve who accepted him, plus a cripple, a whore, a crooked customs officer, and a blind man.

Among the twelve, there was one who sold him out, one who betrayed him three times before a fateful dawn, and another who fell asleep on his shoulder. They were all so ashamed that they began to speak in tongues. To be able to forgive them, he did penance, he didn't eat for forty days, he even washed their feet. When he saw that there was nothing to be done, he rose from the table.

All through that spring so long ago, the whole

city smelled pungent and sweet. It was impossible to mistake the stench for anything else. Scores of decomposing bodies, never found, stayed buried under mountains of brick and grey rubble. Funerals and wreckage.

The population was furious. Everyone saw the earthquake as a curse because the president had ordered the destruction of the Orthodox churches.

After that, cities became systematic, orderly. Flat grey buildings popped up on the scarred cobbles of the old town. Peasants became factory workers, raising chickens on balconies. Spring after spring, small vegetable gardens took root: thyme, parsley, green onions, eggplant, lovage, and a few flowers here and there.

In history textbooks and on maps, the subsoil makes us dream, shakes us with the destiny of geography, the Scythian, Anatolian, Moesian, and Transylvanian microplates. Not satisfied with geological diversity, we even reach for Sanskrit through the language of the Roma.

We don't have the satisfaction of our own natural disaster. Even the earthquake had to be shared with Bulgaria to the south.

In his letters my brother wrote, *No earthquakes here, you never wait in line to buy food. You can say whatever comes into your head without the police taking you away. It's easy to get a passport.* But at the airport my brother also told me not to speak French from France, *they'll hate you.*

Last night, the very night I arrived, there was an earthquake. Six point two on the Richter scale, with the epicentre in the Saguenay region. Little damage, no deaths.

Instead of running to shelter, I called my brother. *You promised me that there wouldn't be earthquakes here!*

My older brother is one of those who know. But now I have a doubt. What if he's not infallible? What would happen to the world? What if he's wrong about the French too?

So, if not French from France, what language gives the orders around here?

Is there one language for day and another for night?

And there was morning, one day.

Second Day, Second Cup of Coffee

This morning, when I wake up, the earth has stopped shaking. Those who know how to make the world go round must have put some oil in the machinery.

There are cockroaches in the kitchen. I've never seen cockroaches before.

Every evening, after the child's bath, when he's asleep, I sprinkle a white powder in the kitchen to kill the roaches. They eat the powder and their bodies dry up. While the child is still asleep, around four o'clock in the morning, I sweep up the dead cockroaches and wash everything three times.

Because of the cockroaches, for the child's sake, every night around four o'clock I become one of those who know.

I have a second coffee; the seven hour time difference.

Both suitcases have to be unpacked. When you leave the country for good, you're allowed two suitcases. My passport reads, in three languages, Romanian, Russian and French, *Titularul acestui paşaport este cetăţean român stabilit in străinătate.* Владелец этого паспорта – Румынский поселились за границей. *Le titulaire de ce passeport est citoyen roumain domicilié à l'étranger.*

Between me and the objects around me a luminous fog set in, the fog of departure.

Two suitcases and the child.

In the suitcases, a large Romanian dictionary, two metres of silk ribbon in the colours of the flag (red, yellow, blue), and my alphabet book are waiting patiently. My mother's recipe book and the Bible are wrapped in clothes.

A few of my father's books, which I got to keep after some struggle: *History Begins at Sumer*, *The Assyrians and the Babylonians*, Rousseau's *Confessions,* and *The Civilization of Ancient Egypt*.

I also have some samples of my mother's adventurous spirit: *The Kon-Tiki Expedition: By Raft Across the South Seas*, *Easter Island*, and a biography of Fridtjof Nansen. Nansen passports—stateless passports—were named after him. I packed mine before I left; you never know.

At the Bucharest airport, the customs officers requisitioned my silver tray with the aperitif glasses, imported from Russia.

They made a show of asking, but they already had their hands on the tray, the vultures.

I also had to leave them some perfume from Germany, and a baby bonnet and teddy bear from France. Like me, they believed that once you get out, everything is easy. In the West, there is an abundance of everything, all the time, everyone has good perfume, everyone wears beautiful jewellery. There is powdered milk and coffee, there are condoms and disposable diapers.

The customs officers at the airport, who see thousands of travellers go by without ever leaving the country themselves, are in limbo, hovering, neither outside nor in.

They also confiscated my gold fountain pen, a gift from my father. Made in China, but I won't forgive them for the pen. I will never forgive them!

There were no winter coats in the suitcases. I land at the end of November, but everything is already buried in snow. There is no way this can be the same planet. The sky is high, the light falls on a tilt, we are on the brow of the Earth.

I call home, three minutes, to say hello to my

parents, who are still over there. My father picks up the phone—when it seems important, it's the father who picks up—and I hear the usual click. They've been listening to our telephone conversations for fifteen years already.

My father and I have a language of our own, subtitled and encoded. It evolved naturally, without a word.

We had nowhere to talk in private and nowhere to hide things. When the secret police came, we would hide our Bibles in the beehives. Fortunately, everyone is afraid of bees, and not every policeman is a beekeeper.

Even in church, week after week, in the front row, the secret police was there, the officer writing down every word. The book of Revelation and the book of Daniel, the prophetic books, as well as the metaphors, caused him serious concern.

He had to visit my father to have the sermons explained to him. Apparently he converted after the revolution.

Don't speak France French. How can you speak French if not from France? It's a mystery. But I don't question the brother, who issued the injunction at the airport. The mystery remains.

I won't ask my brother, especially not over the

phone.

There are no known codes for this new life, for the unusual objects, habits, foods, fruits I don't know and can't name even in my own language.

In the stores, people speak to me in French or English. I'm starting to get used to it.

Between me and my new country, the luminous fog filters the world, dampens sound. In the morning, every gesture and every breath soak into me, weightless and unreal.

The bus drivers' greetings delight me. They're the only ones who say hello, welcome. I want to answer but I can't find a word for the Romanian *bine v-am găsit*. Well done.

Might the French language have inadequacies? For example, this obsession with exceptions, like a starlet's whim.

There is a fog between me and my new life, and there is a weight too, a pressure on my head and shoulders that forces me to lie down.

I feel lawless, like an imposter. In the metro or on the bus, I get up and give up my seat even if there are other spots available.

Others are entitled. What if they see?

I don't speak, so as not to French-from-France. I just say *bonjour*, *merci*.

My brother also told me not to look people in

the face, they don't like to be stared at. It must be a local superstition; you don't take someone's face away when you look at them.

There was evening and there was morning.

The Third Day

Today I bought knitting needles, some wool, sewing needles and thread, scissors, clothespins.

The man-in-waiting, the father of the child, has already bought a hammer, a screwdriver, nails, and a stepladder.

For the child, Lego. Coloured pencils and coloured cereal.

Everything is ready, home, woman, man, child.

I think we can start living.

I used to spend a lot of time back home getting ready to play, setting up a scene, happily preparing the game to come. Chamomile flowers in tiny vases, a tiny carpet cut from a torn rug, a half-melted candle for the illusion of fire, the shadows. Too often, the joyful anticipation of the game remained the only game. We were called to dinner.

I have noticed that life allows too many interruptions.

Packing my suitcases took me at least six months. I would try out different arrangements: what comes out, what goes in, how do you know what will be good and necessary once you're on the outside?

One by one, items were folded into the suitcases, which were never closed. The most difficult thing, after choosing the suitcases themselves, was picking clothes for myself and for the child. On the outside, in the West, people seemed very stylish.

I visited the dressmaker weekly, recutting a dress, having a tailor sew a suit out of some English fabric, having silk shirts made for the child. The finest fabrics were only available on the black market, so a few metres of a piece of a parachute made from Japanese silk, donated by my brother, saved the day.

Night after night I ripped out the straps and seams of the parachute. I thought of the parachutists, the lives saved. My delicate embroidery scissors spared the fabric and snipped the thread.

Then I washed the silk and dyed it with plant dye. The parachute produced two elegant shirts for the child, and a summer dress and a nightgown for me. Each garment was a different colour, our camouflage a success.

The seamstress agrees to be paid partly in honey and coffee.

I also had an evening dress made, black lace lined with orange silk.

My father's store of honey melted away before we knew it.

I was getting ready for the biggest party of my life. In the West, you have to be beautiful, clean, brand new.

You have to rise to the occasion, prove that you belong, you have to deserve your new country.

You have to be more beautiful, cleaner than the legitimate citizens, the blood children. In orphanages only the most beautiful babies are picked. In Ceaușescu's Romania apparently there were orphanages where children were taught to speak French so they could be sold for international adoption.

I always wanted to go to Paris, travel, study, set myself apart.

Me and Samuel Rosenstock. During my high school years, I was part of a literary and artistic circle named after our city's native son, the Tristan Tzara Cenacle.

I read everything I could find about Romanian artists who had studied in Paris. Details about scientists and others are harder to find.

I had a copy of *En français dans le texte*, a handbook of errors and improvements.

I memorized whole passages describing the outlines of cathedrals, the Sorbonne, the banks of the Seine and the book stalls, bohemian life, Montparnasse, the Café de Flore. Songs, too, by the Frenchest of the French, Aznavour, Moustaki, Ferrat, Gainsbourg.

The borders were closed, but I still managed to get to a French-speaking country. And once I'm out, there are no more borders. The vertigo is astounding.

Without borders, I'm afraid of falling into a horizontal abyss.

I'm making an effort to rid myself of anything that might seem Eastern European, just as others try to get rid of their provincialism. My Eastern province.

I recite poems in French. Surprised and euphoric, I reread the decision of the Quebec Ministry of Immigration. They wrote to me from Rome, *After the positive study of your file, we grant you and your child the status of permanent residents.*

I am overjoyed! They want us, we are accepted. And they haven't even seen us yet, or our clothes. I have to be worthy of this trust, I have to live up to it.

I am working even harder on my French. The child knows a few words, some songs and nursery rhymes. He repeats what I say but he doesn't speak much, in any language. He is not yet three years old.

But I find their wording perplexing, *the positive study*.

I can feel the danger close by, the threat. I concentrate on the words, parse the phrase. *The positive study* sticks out in my mind, raising the possibility and peril of a negative study.

What's most unexpected is that this was the result of the very fact of them studying the file. The study was favourable, positive? I find the formulation very cultivated, I mull it over, I savour it.

After I read the letter, the veil of light reappears and settles in permanently. The die has been cast.

★

After months of hemming and hawing, the suitcases are closed. What deserves to be left in and taken out? What should I leave with my parents?

Amid all the indecision, the dictionaries never left the suitcases, and the alphabet book and the history of ancient Egypt. The reference to Egypt was wreaking havoc, the Jewish people wandering in the desert for forty years, miracles happened, there was griping and blasphemy but at the end of the journey, half blessing and half punishment, they had their Canaan, and flowing milk and honey.

Another book never came out of the suitcase —my mother's recipe book, without which I would have faced eternal hunger, me and the whole family.

It's not just any cookbook, it's not some modern, revised, expanded edition. This is the recipe book that was given to her at her wedding and which fed me throughout my childhood. All the festive meals, the convalescent soups, the jokes about botched meals, the culinary expression of every birthday, anniversary, birth, and death are locked in this book.

My mother's recipe book has all the seasons, too—canning. As chief alchemist, she presided over the extraordinary transformations of peppers, eggplants, and tomatoes. Quince, sour cherries, and blueberries submitted to her will and were jarred.

With the ration coupons, for one kilo of sugar per person per month and one litre of oil per adult per month, making preserves was a wonder and a sacrifice.

In the months before she did the canning, we took our coffees without joy or sugar, the precious crystals piling up in the cold room away from covetous eyes and ants.

With my mother's recipe book, a sort of culinary talisman, I staved off starvation.

The dictionaries I kept against oblivion.

Life, my new life, can begin.

There was night and there was day.

The Fourth Day

This morning, those who know how to make the world go round are hiding. When I wake up, everything is humming along as usual.

I always set out eggs, milk, and meat for the child. Between my new life and me, between the husband and me, between me and the objects there is that veil of light, the slightly milky light that rounds out the corners and muffles the sounds.

Everything smells differently here. My skin and my waste smell differently, and so do the days of blood.

For the first time in years I am no longer constipated. I am eating enough. But I can't manage to muster a taste for food. Everything tastes like cardboard.

Through my veil of light, I don't dare look too

closely at the little jars of fruit yogurt. They are lovely and colourful, and they must cost a fortune.

In my country, the less grey and dull something was, the more it cost. I pace around the jar, which I think I can't afford.

My body with its different smells, the air itself, and a weight on my shoulders force me to lie down all the time.

The icy street smells like laundry, my new life smells like laundry, the lobby smells like laundry. This is a purge.

We go for a walk, the child dressed in wool, local wool knitted by me, his pants, his sweater, gloves, scarf, and hat. Walking over the snow, he says his feet feel like glass. His dainty wool booties the colour of fresh butter aren't doing the job. We buy him proper boots, little boy's boots, dark and shapeless. The child is no longer stylish, but he's also no longer cold.

For months and months, I keep the habit of setting out eggs, milk, and meat for the child, and the most beautiful fruit. He eats well, he watches cartoons, and, since he discovered Lego and coloured cereal, he looks after himself.

I look around the apartment. There are no plants, there is no nice furniture. All we have is a tiny balcony overlooking a grey street. Farther down, on the roof of the building next door, the neighbours throw their garbage, such a blight. I make curtains, I discover the common laundry room, which everyone from all the apartments uses. There is still no trace of the bright future.

The child goes to school now, and when I ask him questions in Romanian about his life in French he cries. He doesn't know how to answer me, I get impatient. Words fail him. He's learning life directly in French and his Romanian vocabulary stopped growing around the age of four.

The cockroaches are all dead. I leave those who know to do the night work alone, the necessary work.

They match the emptiness with the emptiness and the fullness with the fullness. They do their work seamlessly.

Day Five

There was evening and there was morning. Between the two I became a woman again.

After three years waiting for my passport, a veil of luminous fog had crept in between me and myself. It was numbing me, I couldn't feel anything, it was preparing me to never see the father of my child again. Never again.

There was far too much finality to be able to leave the country. Passport pages only open outward. It's more of an exit ticket, a safe conduct really, than a passport.

Twenty Years After by Alexandre Dumas was an extraordinary discovery. A gift for my brother on his fifteenth birthday, from our mother. When I was eight years old, I presumed it was forbidden (in Romanian the title means *After Twenty*), so I read it in secret.

D'Artagnan's note, signed by Richelieu, that masterpiece of diplomacy and cunning, comes to mind. *It is by my order and for the good of the state that the bearer of this has done what he has done.*

Never again, and the endless wait. There were summons from the secret police, with or without the baby, to try to dissuade me from leaving the country. That was before the passport.

The secret police must have studied Kafka and the Surrealists carefully.

To get a passport, it was implied that you had to submit a number of documents. Proof that you do not own a house on the territory of the Socialist Republic, proof that you do not own a radio on the territory of the Socialist Republic, proof that you do not own land on the territory of the Socialist Republic and that you renounce any future inheritance, and proof that you do not own a typewriter on the territory of the Socialist Republic.

The serial numbers of typewriters were registered with the state and the records filed with the central authorities.

And each declaration or certificate had to be secured in a different place at some random time at the discretion of the issuers in question. Taxes had to be remitted, numerous seals obtained, stamps purchased. Everyone expected a bribe, coffee, cartons of foreign cigarettes, foreign alcohol. Sometimes you'd find out the rules had changed, *come back next week.*

And the following week, two or three additional signatures would be required. Instead of one packet of coffee, suddenly three bags of coffee packaged abroad was the going rate. We called it foreign coffee, even though no coffee bean had ever sprouted in the country.

Coffee became a bargaining chip, like ingots. Packets of coffee were passed around, from hand to hand, the shiny gold-coloured corners of the packages creased and worn over time.

There was some coffee in the grocery stores, made from barley or chickpeas, and from chicory, like during the war. To dress up this second-rate coffee for guests, a single real coffee bean was left to float on the surface. In those wartime days with no war, we were issued ration coupons for milk, oil, sugar, and bread. Meat was only available on the black market. Political jokes, not least about food, ran rampant—a gentle sedition, even at the cost of being denounced. Making fun of the system was a way to retain some semblance of dignity, to feel like you were still in control of your destiny.

Demoralized and tired, most of us resisted the call to inform on our parents, neighbours, and brothers. Not everyone resists, or they resist no longer. The people become the enemy of the people.

★

The second suitcase brims with superfluous things, clothing that was too fancy or not warm enough. It's November, emigration day five. Outside, the landscape is frozen with snow, and inside, in the tiny apartment, I keep the cockroaches to myself. The child hasn't seen them. I report to those who know.

The borders are sealed from the outside too. It's too dangerous to return home, and too expensive. This new, economical exile takes up all the space: working, saving, studying.

★

Paris seems farther than ever. I don't quite understand the French I hear.

I'm getting used to it. Aftershocks of discouragement.

Beckon other fairies over to your own cradle,

in another language, to ward off fate, change your destiny.

Though I don't know it at the time, I write my last poem in Romanian, "*Seve deturnate*," sap diverted.

I don't speak, I mustn't speak French from France. I read, I'm getting used to it.

My country is the French language, and I travel there in books. From time to time, I have to step out, I have to go back to school, my diplomas have been beheaded. I thought I had abolished capital punishment.

The axe falls very quickly. Secondary five, locksmith. In Romania I'd finished classical high school, I took Latin and even atomic and nuclear physics.

But I can't formulate a complete sentence in French, I can't argue with them, I can't ask, I don't understand, they don't understand.

Still I ask to be registered for French *comme tout le monde*, not for non-speakers, the same lessons as everyone else. I want to learn.

Every day I have headaches. The grande dame is ruthless. Everything takes place in French, all the time.

In despair, I fall back on writing poetry. Like the little pots of yogurt, long, well-turned sentences remain out of reach.

I read, I read, but much more slowly than in Romanian. I feel humiliated, demoted.

Square One

Hello my name is. I am studying letters,
metres of language, letters squared.
I am studying letters, degrees Celsius,
points along the Richter scale, and beauty.
I am studying letters, word processing, and hopelessness.
I am studying letters, left feet, heart dotting the i.
I look forward to meeting sentences.

On The Sixth Day

There was night and there was day.

The weekdays are clumped together like a bouquet of flowers, their stems clutched together by morning's hand. When evening comes, swollen with work, tears, and heat, the days unfold like a fan.

French tastes like migraine.

And always there is a veil of light between me and the world. I sit on the words and I roll my *r*s, but I manage to make myself understood. My French is almost phonetic.

What gives me the most trouble is the gender of nouns. My universe has been flipped upside down: *rose*, *huile*, and *épaule* are feminine, though I used to know roses, oil, and shoulders as masculine, while *cœur*, *banc*, *visage*, and *pays* have become masculine, where before hearts, benches, faces, and countries were feminine or neuter.

This betrayal doesn't suit me at all. You just have to memorize it, and people ask you to repeat yourself, start again, rephrase please.

There are people who correct you, constantly.

She's so distant and ruthless, but I've loved her for too long, I've been taming her, I've been asking her for mercy. It's a desperate, unrequited love.

I don't speak French. I park myself on my sentences, unyielding.

They call me *la dame au dictionnaire*. Dumas's *La dame aux camélias* I know, and Chekhov's *The Lady With the Dog*, but the lady with the dictionary... As an accessory, it seems a bit unwieldy.

I commit crimes of dissonance, crimes against French.

People always ask me where I come from, *Oh, Nadia Comăneci, oh, Ceaușescu*. And *Oh, it's good here,* chez nous.

Now I wake up mostly on the French side. I read, and read, and read. I haven't won the race yet, but now I can read almost as fast as I do in Romanian.

It took me six months.

And I'm writing.

Parallel

On the little-known continent of the French language
I stand. Here is Victor Hugo, some people claim,
or Molière, Verlaine. Others say Saint-Exupéry or Prévert.
They're wrong, just as they were wrong about America.
My new continent is the French language,
lonely island with no memories or childhood,
unrequited through and through.

On my new continent I live poorly,
below the threshold of the translatable.
I have no land of my own to nibble on, take
a bite of sadness. No friend—port, storm,
lifeline. From Nelligan and Verlaine,
Prévert and Vigneault, Félix Leclerc and all's fair, slowly
slowly I build my parallel continent.

Day Seven and Everything After

The long, interminable plane trip with the child will always have a before and an after—BT, before trip, and AT, after. It's hard to believe how different it is. BT and AT, six of one. For the last time, I write the month in Roman numerals. 25 XI 1988.

Except, of course, when I date the letters I send home, out of consideration for those who still write dates in Roman numerals. They haven't figured out that Roman numerals are dead letters. It's not the kind of information you learn by listening to Radio Europa Libera or Vocea Americii.

The child, with his Lego and cartoons and his colourful cereal, is asked over to a friend's house. The parents are not invited.

We always emigrate for the children, that's what we say.

We look elsewhere for the bright future we've been given a glimpse of, the future for which we have suffered, planted trees, won prizes, held the flag, shot at targets, done our homework by candlelight. The bright future to which we submitted our self-criticism.

It seems logical to me that I would run into a few inconveniences before getting there, and once again I accept it—for me, not for the child.

The cockroaches in the apartment are anecdotal. There must be some in Paris too. I've read about it, somewhere, roaches in foreign students' garrets. I'd never seen them before because I hadn't travelled enough, maybe. Cockroaches, the cold, the noise, the cramped living conditions—it's all part of a certain bohemian atmosphere, isn't it?

I'm out of line, out of lineage. Out of my continent too.

Genealogy creaks and twists. When the time comes, smuggled seeds shoot up with a clamour.

Every spring, in April, my father calls me. *Ce mai faci Moaca, ești bine? Te-am sunat sa-ti spun c-a înflorit liliacul!* How are you, little one? I called to tell you that your lilac is in bloom. Around Orthodox Easter, the lilac is stepping out.

The secret police who listen to our telephone conversations are now officially forbidden, but

night the earth shook—a technical issue or a superhuman error. Since last night, other continents have been taking shape.

And He rested on the seventh day from all His work which He had done.

That was twenty-eight years ago.

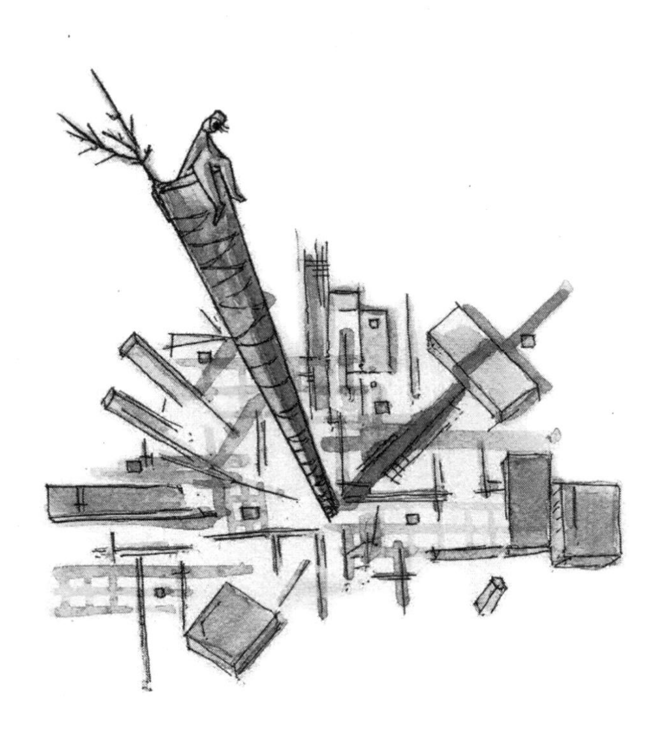

The still point

Envoi

I stepped back in order to write, and to make an offering to the big city, a bone dug up from my memories.

I'm moored in the city, it's my pivot, my equilibrium, my salvation.

So many times I almost lost my footing, I got sucked in, caught up by the city and the outside world, sped-up and specific, I was strained by its electric storms.

I tucked the weight of childhood into my shoes so I wouldn't fall. In the left shoe, stones from the miraculous river, with its slippery, shimmery fish. In the right, the heavy smell of the barn, the steaming milk, the pealing of the bells and the hooves of the cows returning alone from the pasture.

I like the pages on the right, their quiet stability,

somewhere between faith and foundation. The pages on the left can be skimmed quickly. The writing on the left-hand page is shaky, forced, the letters are unsteady and off-balance.

The pages on the left are a bad time, a time to get through.

But the words on the right...

Vaudreuil-sur-le-Lac
August 2016

Acknowledgements

Thank you to my first readers, Robert and Danielle, and Claire and André, and to Luc, Michel and Monique for their care and friendship.

To outstanding proofreaders Roxane and Véronique. To Rachida Azdouz for her intercultural spark. To Andy for his comments.

To the student strike, which allowed me to meet Pascale Noizet.

To Iulia and her unshakeable faith.

To Pierre Foglia, an inspiration to those he loves and to the other fish he has to fry.

To my father, his books and his bees. To my

mother, the fairy witch.

To Frédéric, who only reads published things.

To Pinel, the woman, not the institute, who gave me permission to live among the not-so-crazy.

To my White Knight for his unfailing enthusiasm.

To Jeannot Clair, my French publisher, who supported me with his panoramic intelligence and sensitive science.

Thanks to my travel accomplice and illustrator, and the child, Edwin.

My gratitude also to the universe for introducing me to Dame Katia Grubisic, for her human and poetic talents, and for the gift of words made to measure. *Vivat*!

My thanks to Linda Leith, a woman of heart and vision, who breathed new life to *Le cimetière des abeilles*, and to Leila Marshy, for carrying and ferrying this project.

Some sections of the original French version of this novel were published previously: "Panoptique" appeared as "Panopticon" in *Contre-jour* (32, February 2014), and "Casting" appeared in *Virages* (67, summer 2014). The poem "Parallèles" appeared in *Former des adultes en milieu multiethnique*, edited by Monique Ouellette (Beauchemin, 1995).